NOSE PICKERS from OUTER SPACE

Gordon Korman

Illustrated by **Victor Vaccaro**

64% OF PEOPLE admit to picking their NOSES—0% OF tHEM are FrOM OUTEr SPACE.

SCHOLASTIC INC.

New York Toronto London Auckland Sydney
Mexico City New Delhi Hong Kong

For Jay Howard Korman,
the NEWEST Earthling
—G.K.

For My Father, with
affection and admiration
—V.V.

ISBN 0-439-14894-4

12 11 10 9 8 7 6 5 4 3 2 1   9/9 0 1 2 3 4/0

Printed in the U.S.A.   40

First Scholastic printing, September 1999

CONTENTS

Chapter 1
NERD ALERT

✳ DEVIN HUNTER'S RULES OF COOLNESS ✳

> ☛ **Rule 1:** Don't ever act excited—even when you're excited.

I kept saying it over and over to myself at the airport.

"What are you mumbling?" my mother asked me.

I didn't answer. That was because of ☛ **Rule 6: In public, NEVER show that you have a mother.**

It was one of the most important of my rules of coolness, along with ☛ **Rule 9: Broccoli is for losers,** and ☛ **Rule 27: Don't let anyone sew name tags on your underwear.**

But back to Rule 1. I didn't want it to show, but inside I was totally psyched. We were here to pick up my exchange buddy. That was a pretty big thing in our school.

Most of the fourth-graders signed up for the National Student Exchange Program. Your exchange buddy was a kid from another state. He or she would come to live at your house for a month, and go to school with you as a guest student.

Joey Petrillo already had a great exchange buddy, Cody. Cody was from Texas. He lived on a real ranch. He could rope and tie a calf in less than ten seconds. And Calista Bernstein's buddy, Wanda, came from California. She dressed like a supermodel and even wore makeup!

Come to think of it, all the exchange buddies had turned out to be pretty cool. That's why I was so excited about meeting Stan. Was he a star quarterback? A Nintendo master? A laugh-a-minute class clown?

Mom checked her watch. "Where could he be?"

Good question. All the passengers were off Flight 407. They were picking up their suitcases at the baggage claim.

Suddenly, the luggage carousel groaned to a halt. The lights flickered once, and then the whole airport went dark.

"Stay close to me," ordered Mom in the gloom. "It's a power failure."

The words were barely out of her mouth when the lights came on again. The carousel sprang back to life, and more luggage came down the slide. Out rolled a steamer trunk, a garment bag, two duffles, and a *person!* He tumbled down the chute, hit the carousel, and started circling like he was a suitcase.

TALK abOUT EXCESS baggagE.

Baggage Claim B

I was so shocked that I broke Rule 6.

"Mom, did you see that?"

But she was looking the other way.

A shiny silver travel bag came down and bonked the guy on the head. He picked it up, jumped off the carousel, and landed at our feet.

What a nerd this kid was! He had a crew cut, and big thick glasses that made his eyes look like fried eggs. Worst of all, he was wearing a tie!

Didn't he know about ☞ **Rule 21:** No ties? His pants were too short! His sleeves were too long! I think his belt was up under his arms somewhere.

"Beat it, kid," I whispered. "I'm looking for my exchange buddy."

"You must be Devin Hunter," said the nerd with a little munchkin voice.

Oh no, I prayed to myself. **Please don't be Stan.**

He nodded, grinning. Even his teeth were nerdy. "I'm Stan."

Mom took his suitcase and smiled at him. "What's your last name, Stan? In the letter from the exchange program, there must have been a mistake. It looked something like Mflxnys."

He beamed. "That's me. Stan Mflxnys."

M f l x n y s ? I was going to have to introduce this guy around school. Everybody would think I had a mouthful of gravel!

"Welcome, Stan," said Mom. "The car's just outside—"

"Hold it!" I choked. "This could be the wrong Stan Mflxnys!"

5

It wasn't. He had all the papers to prove he was the right person.

"Thank you for hosting me," he said stiffly. "May the Crease be with you."

May the *what?*

My mom giggled. "Oh, Stan. You're so full of fun."

Fun wasn't the word I was thinking of. Try *baloney*.

It wasn't fair. In a world of cool exchange buddies, I got the dweeb.

Chapter 2
STAN FROM PAN

When Mom put the suitcase in the trunk of our Honda, Stan tried to climb in there with it.

I stared at the guy. "Haven't you ever seen a car before?"

"Only in pictures," he told me, dead serious.

My mother laughed and laughed. "You're such a joker, Stan."

But I didn't think he was joking. I was starting to think he was crazy. "Where are you from, the Moon?" I asked.

He frowned at me. "There are no intelligent life forms on Earth's Moon. I, Stan, am from Pan."

"The letter said you were from Chicago," my mother put in.

"Right. Of course," Stan amended. "Pan is—outside Chicago."

I groaned. Stan from Pan. **I had to make up a new rule of coolness—something about your name rhyming with your hometown.** I'm against it. It sounds dumb.

When we got home, Mom and I showed Stan up to my room. All my stuff was pushed to one side so we could move in the extra bed.

"That's where you sleep," I told him. "You know, unless you prefer the furnace room or the garage or something."

"Don't be rude," Mom said sharply. "Stan, you get yourself unpacked. Then come and meet the rest of the family."

Mom and I started downstairs. Suddenly, I heard footsteps behind me. It was Stan!

I stared at him. "You're supposed to unpack first."

"Yes."

"So do it!"

"I, Stan, have completed the task."

"You're finished? No way!" I ran back up. My jaw dropped. Shirts hung in the closet; pants were folded in the drawer. A whole shelf of books sat on top of the dresser. There was a dartboard on the wall, and a bearskin rug on the floor. All this out of one small silver suitcase! And he did it in two seconds! **What was going on here?**

I checked out the clothes. They were all the same. I mean, identical. He had twenty black ties with white polka dots. Fifteen dress shirts. And—what was this? A Chicago Bulls basketball jersey—number twenty-three!

Hooray! Something normal! I grabbed it and ran down to the family room.

Mom was introducing Stan to my father, my older brother, Roscoe, and my kid sister, Lindsay.

I barged right in and waved the jersey in Stan's face. "You've got to wear this to school tomorrow! It's the only decent thing you own!"

"I, Stan, never wear that shirt," he said seriously. "It's a gift from a dear friend."

Roscoe put an arm around Stan's wimpy shoulders. "Awesome, you're a Bulls fan! Me, too. There's a game on tonight. We can watch it together."

"Acceptable," Stan told him.

Did you catch that? *Acceptable?* He talked like he'd swallowed a dictionary! But my

family didn't even notice. They thought he was
great.

Even Fungus, our cocker spaniel, loved Stan.
Fungus, who hates everybody, jumped up on his
lap and barked at him. Stan looked right into our
dog's eyes and barked back.

I don't have a rule of coolness about talking to dogs. I didn't think I needed one. But there was a whole woof-woof conversation going on!

All at once, Stan threw back his head and laughed.

"What's so funny?" I asked, disgusted.

"Fungus knows a lot of knock-knock jokes," he told me.

"He's a dog!" I said through clenched teeth.

He nodded. "With an excellent sense of humor."

KNOCK KNOCK. WHO'S THERE? WOOF.

It was after midnight when I finally figured out what was really wrong with that conversation. **Nobody had told Stan that our dog's name was Fungus!**

I went over to the other bed. Stan was snoring. Naturally, the dweeb couldn't snore like a normal person. The noise that came out of him sounded more like the hum of a microwave oven.

I shook him awake. "How did you know?" I demanded. "How did you know the name of our dog?"

"He told me," Stan mumbled.

"My dad? Roscoe?"

"No. Fungus."

And, no matter how hard I shook him, I couldn't wake him up again.

Chapter 3

EIGHTY·FIVE THOUSAND LIGHT·YEARS

☛ **Rule 11:** If you hang out with a dweeb, people are going to think you're a dweeb, too.

That was the problem with bringing Stan from Pan to school. It would take about five seconds for everybody to figure out that this was the biggest nerd in town.

So on the way to Clearview Elementary, I gave him a crash course in how to be cool.

"Listen, Stan," I said carefully. "This place is different from your school back in Chicago—"

"Pan," Stan corrected.

"Right. Pan. What I'm trying to say is this: around here, dogs bark at people. People don't bark at dogs. You don't want everyone to think you're—you know—a dweeb or something. You have to be cool."

"Not necessarily," he told me. "If I'm cool, I, Stan, can put on something called a sweater and warm right up."

All right . . . Plan B. "Stan, don't open your mouth at all. School rules. Mr. Slomin is big on quiet."

But as soon as I said it, along came Tanner Phelps and his exchange buddy, a real cool-looking kid with red hair and sunglasses that were mirrors.

"Hey, Devin, I want you to meet Sam Purvis. His soccer team was Minnesota state champs last year."

I burned with jealousy. Sam really was a fantastic soccer player. While we were talking, he was bouncing a ball off his head. I'll bet he could keep it up there for hours! I'll also bet he never barked at anybody's dog. Not once in his life!

"Hi, Sam," I greeted.

Both boys were looking at Stan, taking in the fried-egg eyes and the polka-dot tie.

"Aren't you going to introduce us to your buddy?" asked Tanner.

"Oh," I said. "This is Stan—" I dropped my voice and mumbled, "Mflxnys."

"Could you repeat that?" requested Soccer Sam. "It sounded like you just said 'Mflxnys.'"

My dweeb stepped forward. "Correct. Stan Mflxnys. May the Crease be with you." He shook hands with both of them. The soccer ball hit the ground and bounced away.

"Gee." Tanner's eyes narrowed. "That's a pretty weird name you've got there, kid."

Stan was surprised. "Really? Where I, Stan, come from, the phone book has a full page of us Mflxnyses."

"He's from Pan," I said quickly. "It's near Chicago. Stan's a big Chicago Bulls fan."

Sam looked interested. "How far is your house from the United Center where the Bulls play?"

Stan thought it over. "Not far. You make a left on Third Street, go down five blocks—"

Sam came a step closer. The twin mirrors of his sunglasses flashed in Stan's face. Suddenly, the dweeb's eyes crossed. "Approximately eighty-five thousand light-years," he finished in that munchkin voice.

The bell rang. It saved my life.

Class 4C was pretty crowded. We had our regular twenty-three kids, plus fourteen exchange buddies.

Mr. Slomin started the day by asking all the

visitors to introduce themselves. Sam gave a soccer demonstration. Wanda from Hollywood talked about the time she and her family ate next to Steven Spielberg in a restaurant. Cody made a lariat out of someone's jump rope and lassoed Mr. Slomin. It was pretty funny. But I couldn't enjoy it, because I knew Stan was up next.

"I'm Stan from Pan," said my exchange buddy. He almost had to talk around his tie. It was on so tight that it stuck straight up in front of his face. "I, Stan, am a very average youngster. My

hobbies are knitting, doing homework, going to the dentist, and cleaning my room."

I wanted to crawl under my desk.

Joey nudged me from behind. "I pity the poor jerk who has to be buddies with *that* nerd."

What could I do? I agreed with Joey. I pitied myself.

"My buddy is Devin Hunter," Stan announced. "I, Stan, first met him yesterday when he and his mother picked me up at the airport."

Mr. Slomin jumped to his feet. "The airport? There was a UFO sighting at the airport yesterday! Did you see anything?"

Mr. Slomin was totally into UFOs—unidentified flying objects. At first, it was fun to have a teacher who talked about visitors from outer space. But waiting for aliens can be pretty boring, especially when they never show up.

"I, Stan, observed nothing," said Stan.

UFOs weren't just a hobby with Mr. Slomin. He was nuts on the subject. It was enough to turn a normal adult into the weirdest teacher at school.

"Think harder," he urged. "From an airplane

you would have a perfect chance to spot a spaceship or a flying saucer."

Stan shook his head. "Sorry, Mr. Slomin."

But when Mr. Slomin was talking about UFOs, he was like a bloodhound. "What about your fellow passengers? You know, the other Pannites on the plane?"

Stan frowned. "Pannites? Oh, no, we're not called Pannites. People from Pan are known as Pants."

That did it. The whole class howled with

laughter. It came on a tidal wave, washing away all talk about UFOs.

Then, just when I thought things couldn't get any worse, I looked up at my exchange buddy. There he stood, in front of the whole class—
with his finger up his nose!

Question: What could be worse than a nerd exchange buddy?

Answer: A nerd nose picker.

This bOOK is rEaLLY
ENGROSSINg!

Chapter 4
HAPPY 147TH BIRTHDAY

"Listen, Stan," I said at lunch. "You're not a very cool guy. I can live with that. But you've got to stop picking your nose. It's worse than just the uncoolest thing in the world. It's gross!"

Stan was outraged. "Pants are not nose pickers."

"I saw you!" I insisted. "The whole class saw you! You were up there to the second knuckle!"

Tanner and Sam plunked their trays down opposite us. Calista and Wanda took the seats beside them.

"Can anybody sit here?" giggled Calista. "Or is it just for Pants?"

"I'm *wearing* pants," added Tanner. "Does that count?"

"Please join us," invited Stan. "May the Crease be with you."

"The *crease*?" echoed Calista. "You mean the crease in your . . . *pants*?"

Everybody laughed, even Stan. I think the poor guy believed he was popular, instead of the laughingstock of the fourth grade. I'll bet my face was bright red.

"Well, I'm starved." I picked up my slice of pizza.

Stan picked up his, too. **And he took a big bite—*out of the paper plate!***

I started to choke. Before our horrified eyes, Stan munched happily until the plate was gone. Then he ate his napkin. He started to nibble at the plastic tray, but shook his head. "Stale," he decided. He wiped his mouth with his pizza and threw it in the garbage. "Delicious!" he burped happily.

"Oooh, gross!" exclaimed Wanda. "Stan ate paper!"

"Devin, where did you find this guy?" Tanner hissed. "He's a nut-job!"

I had to change the subject. I wracked my

brain. What does everybody love to talk about? And then it came to me.

"My birthday is next month," I announced loudly. "November twenty-seventh. I'll be ten. Double digits."

It worked!

"I'm already ten," said Calista. "It's no big deal."

"My birthday is on Christmas Eve," Sam piped up. "I hate that."

"It's better than July," put in Wanda. "All your friends are at camp. There's nobody around to come to your party." She pushed away her salad and popped open her makeup compact. She

dabbed at her nose with the powder puff. "How about you, Stan? When's your birthday?"

"Well, Wanda—" Stan turned to answer her and found himself staring into the mirror of her compact. His eyes crossed. "When the North Star passes through the constellation of Scorpio, I, Stan, will be 147."

Calista gave me a shove. "Devin—"

Like it was my fault that I got the worst exchange buddy of all time!

"He's just kidding," I mumbled. "He's a great kidder."

But deep down, I knew there was something very weird about this guy.

Chapter 5

THE GREAT
DISHWASHING MYSTERY

This called for drastic action, and I was just the guy to take it. I let Stan read my Rules of Coolness notebook. I'd never let anybody see it before. No one knew it existed.

I even added a few special rules aimed just at him: ☞ **Don't cross your eyes unless it's part of a joke.** And: ☞ **If homework is your hobby, shut up about it.** And of course: ☞ **No nose picking.**

It wasn't easy. Stan kept me on my toes making sure the rules were up to date. For example, Rule 44 started out: ☞ **Don't eat paper.** But Stan went after paper the way a dog digs in a flower bed. He couldn't help himself! I had to change the rule to: ☞ **Don't eat paper, cardboard, phone books, catalogs, packing cartons, or the mail.** And still there were teeth marks in my *World Book Encyclopedia*.

At school, Stan was a total loss. The kids called him every name you could think of: Stan-Pan, Pan-Stan, Stan from Pan the Panty Man, and Stan-Stan Moo Goo Gai Pan.

The nose picking jokes were the worst:

"Hey, Stan, if you find anything up there, I'll split it with you, fifty-fifty!"

"What are you doing—drilling for oil?"

Oh sure, everyone's a comedian . . .

"Shake hands? I don't think so!"

They laughed at him, which meant they were also laughing at me. While exchange buddies like Sam, Wanda, and Cody were welcomed like movie stars, Stan and I were treated like we smelled bad. I didn't get invited to Ralph O'Malley's party because nobody wanted a nose picker too close to the cake. To be honest, I couldn't blame them.

"Sorry, Devin," Ralph whispered to me in gym class. "I was kind of afraid he would eat the streamers."

What could I do? I added *streamers* to Rule 44.

Yeah, school was rough. But I have to say, home was worse. Nobody believed me when I told them how weird Stan was.

"But Mom, he's a nose picker!"

"Oh, stop it," she scolded me. "You've been mean to poor Stan ever since he arrived. Everyone has a couple of bad habits."

"Does everyone eat paper?" I challenged.

"Oh, come now," she scoffed. "A lot of people chew paper. It isn't very nice, but it's not the end of the world."

I was getting desperate. "He doesn't chew it! He *eats* it! It's his favorite food! He throws away his lunch and chows down on the bag! Yesterday I caught him sneaking the newspapers out of the recycling bin! He's crazy!"

Boy, was Mom ever mad! You'd think Stan was her real son, and I was the idiot who had come out of the baggage chute at the airport. She put me on dishwashing duty for the whole rest of the week.

Scraping plates and loading the dishwasher is the job I hate second most in the world. The worst is *un*loading the dishwasher and putting everything away. And I was stuck doing both for three entire days. I had to get out of it!

I found Stan in my kid sister Lindsay's room, playing Barbies with her. Every time I think he's hit the bottom of the dweeb ocean, he manages to sink a few more feet.

I took him aside. "Great news, Stan. Mom's put me in charge of the dishwasher. And I'm going to let you help."

"Don't do it, Stan!" cried Lindsay. "He's just using you to—*oomff!*" I quickly stuck my hand over her mouth.

"So, what do you say?" I asked Stan.

"I, Stan, will assist you," he declared like he was Superman, about to save the world.

It's a bird . . .
It's a PLaNE . . .
It's SuPErpicKEr!

Dinner was spaghetti with meat sauce, so the plates were covered in gunk. During dessert, I leaned over to Stan and whispered, "Let's make a race out of it."

As soon as Mom and Dad were gone from the table, I yelled, "Ready, set, go!" Then I sprinted down to the basement to hide while he did all the work. Okay, so I'm not such a swell guy.

But the next minute, I heard Roscoe taking him to watch the Bulls game on TV.

I rushed back upstairs. "No! No! No!" I dropped my voice to a whisper. "What about the dishes? The race?"

Stan beamed at me. "I, Stan, was victorious," he announced with pride.

"You mean you *won*? No way!"

He led me into the kitchen. The dishwasher was empty.

"Aw, Stan! You haven't even started loading it yet!"

He opened the cupboard. The dishes were sparkling clean and neatly put away. The glasses and cutlery were all in their places. The counter was clear, and the floor gleamed. Even the garbage had been taken out.

"But that's impossible!" I exploded. "The dishwasher alone takes half an hour! You've been at this for thirty seconds! What did you do?"

"I, Stan, beat you," he chortled, and went back to the basketball game.

Don't get me wrong. I was thrilled that the dishes were all done. But this was kind of creepy!

So the next day after dinner, I didn't go hide in the basement. I stuck around to see how Stan could do forty-five minutes of cleanup in thirty seconds.

I was walking into the kitchen with an armload

of dessert plates. And then *poof!*

They disappeared.

"What the—"

And there was Stan, standing in the middle of our spotless kitchen, grinning at me. "I, Stan, win again."

I threw open the cupboard and gawked. There were the plates that had vanished from my hands. Five seconds ago they had been smeared with chocolate cake. Now they were washed, dried, and stacked.

I pointed at Stan. **"You've got helpers, right? A bunch of guys hiding in the pantry?"**

Even while I was saying it, I knew it was stupid. A hundred people couldn't do the dishes that fast. And they definitely couldn't make my armload of plates go *poof!*

On Friday night, I had to stick to Stan like glue. I followed him into the kitchen. I followed him out of the kitchen. I even followed him to the bathroom. When he emerged, munching on a tissue, there I was.

"Do you require something of me, Devin?" he asked innocently.

"I'm not letting you out of my sight for one second!" I snarled. "Even if it kills me, I'm going to see how you do those dishes so fast!"

He seemed surprised. "But Devin, the dishes have already been done."

"*What?*" I sprinted back to the kitchen. Another perfect job. "Oh, no! Not again!"

When did he do all that work? I watched every move he made! I didn't take my eyes off the guy. The one time I looked away was when he stuck his finger up his nose. Who could blame me? Nose picking is not a spectator sport!

It dawned on me like a sunrise. It was the nose! Stan always said he wasn't picking it.

> It's NOT WHETHER YOU WIN OR LOSE. It's HOW YOU PICK THAT COUNTS!

What if he was telling the truth? Maybe he was doing something else—something that only *looked* like picking.

After all, noses were meant for smelling, breathing, and blowing. They were there to perch your glasses on. Nobody said anything about doing the dishes!

There was only one explanation for all this: my exchange buddy had a magic nose!

Chapter 6

NOT YOUR AVERAGE, RUN·OF·THE·MILL SCHNOZ

"Good night, Devin," called my mother. "Good night, Stan. Sleep well."

I got into bed. But sleep wasn't even part of the plan. How could I sleep, with that nose only a few feet away in the other bed?

As usual, Stan was out like a light the second his head hit the pillow. You could tell by his microwave-oven snoring. I jumped out of bed, tiptoed over, and peered down at my exchange buddy. Just as I suspected! The power hum was coming right from his magic nose!

I took out my mini-flashlight and shone the beam at Stan's schnoz. It looked like a pretty regular nose to me. I had to get a look inside. But how?

Then it came to me. My mom had one of those mirrors—the kind that magnifies everything. I ran for the bathroom.

Oh, no! Roscoe was taking one of his famous five-hour showers! I could hear him soaping and whistling.

If you interrupt my brother in the shower, you automatically start World War Three. But I needed that mirror. I decided to take a chance.

I eased the bathroom door open.

Squeak!

Behind the shower curtain, the whistling stopped. "Who's there?" Roscoe demanded.

I snatched the mirror up from the vanity and made a break for it. The door shut with a too-loud snap.

"That better not be you, Devin!" came a growl from inside.

In the hall, I watched as the mirror unfogged. My own face appeared, giant-size. Perfect. This would be as good as a microscope right up Stan's nostrils.

I ran back into my room. My swan dive into bed would have won me an Olympic medal.

Angry footsteps started down the hall. I shoved the mirror under my pillow and started to work on my I've-been-asleep-for-hours look.

The door opened a crack. "Devin?" came a whisper.

I kept my mouth shut. Stan snored on.

"Did you just barge in on me?"

But a world-class faker is impossible to catch. I faked sleep so well that I even dozed off for real. The next thing I knew, Roscoe was gone, and it was after two in the morning.

Silently, I crept out of bed. It was time to learn the secret of my exchange buddy's magic schnoz.

I crouched over Stan and carefully rested the mirror on his upper lip. Then I shone my mini-flashlight into his nostrils, and peered down at the glass.

My heart nearly leaped out my throat. Now, I'm not a nose expert. But you don't have to be a genius to realize that **this was not your average, run-of-the-mill schnoz.** The inside of Stan's nose was all shiny, silver and chrome. There were hundreds of tiny buttons, switches, dials, and blinking colored lights.

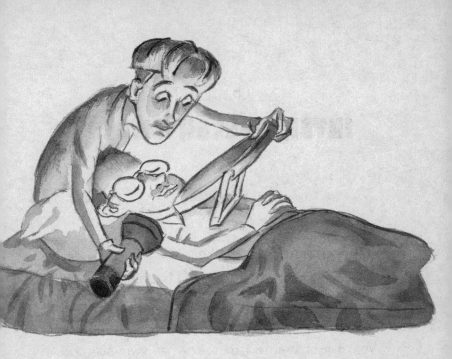

No wonder Stan snored a power hum. I was amazed he didn't have to plug himself into the wall like a toaster! This nose wasn't magic at all! It was—

"A machine!" I blurted.

"A computer," corrected an all-too-familiar munchkin voice.

Chapter 7
INTERSTELLAR DWEEBS

Oh, no! Stan was awake!

"I can explain everything," I babbled. "I was . . . uh . . . *jealous* because you've got such a great nose. And you know how you're always picking it? Well, I just wanted to see what was so *good* in there—"

Stan didn't say a word. He just lay there with his eyes crossed.

That always happened when my exchange buddy looked into a mirror. It was like he was hypnotized.

"What kind of guy has a computer up his nose?" I mumbled to myself.

"All Pants have nasal processors," Stan replied, still cross-eyed.

"Yeah, right," I snorted. "You expect me to believe there's a whole town outside Chicago where everybody has a computer in his schnoz? **I mean, I've heard of laptops, but *nosetops?***"

"Pan isn't a town," he told me. "It's a planet."

"Aw, come on, Stan! Quit fooling around—"

All at once, his nose began to twitch. A high-pitched beeping sound came out of his nostrils. I checked Mom's mirror. The blinking lights were going crazy, flashing like a nervous Christmas tree. Switches flipped. Dials whizzed like tiny pinwheels. A miniature satellite dish wheeled around and around. What was going on in there?

A superpowered light shone through the curtains. I dropped the mirror and ran to the window. Our backyard was as bright as a summer afternoon!

Suddenly, a large gleaming object descended out of the sky. It was shaped like a giant stop sign—flat with eight sides. It was the color of aluminum foil covered in the same kind of blinking lights that were up Stan's nose. A flashing neon pipe on the top puffed a shower of sparks.

You couldn't spend a whole year in Mr. Slomin's class without recognizing what this was.

"A UFO!" I rasped, terrified. I threw myself to the floor and scrambled under the bed. Okay, it wasn't very cool. But there was no rule of coolness about how to act when a spaceship is landing in your backyard.

That's when I saw Stan's feet. He was getting up!

> INSTRUCTIONS FOR AN ALIEN INVASION: MAKE LIKE A TREE AND GET THE HECK OUT OF THERE.

"Hide!" I whispered urgently.

A hand reached down and picked the mirror up off the floor. The bare feet began to walk away.

"Stan! Come back!" I hissed. "There's a UFO out there! A real UFO!"

I heard the door close. Desperately, I tried to picture the pamphlet from the National Student Exchange Program. It said you had to house and feed your buddy and take him to school with you. There was nothing about rescuing him from space invaders.

I shook my head to clear it. What was I thinking? Dweeb or not, Stan was my buddy. I had to look out for him—no matter what he had up his nose.

I crept out from under the bed, got up on my knees, and peered over the windowsill. The spaceship's lights were dim. It was parked in our yard, right in Dad's prize flower garden.

A tiny black dot appeared in the wall of the craft. It grew larger until it had become a big round door. A staircase descended, and a red carpet unfurled to the petunia bed. Two aliens strolled down and stood at the foot of the steps, waiting.

At least, I *thought* they were aliens. They looked totally human. To be honest, they looked kind of like Stan, only older—the same crew cuts, white shirts, and ties knotted so tight that they stuck out in front.

In a flash, I understood everything. It was like all the pieces of a puzzle had been put together at the same instant. Mr. Slomin's UFO at the airport! It was Stan! I didn't have to save Stan from aliens because Stan was an alien, too!

It was all true! Pan really *was* a planet, not a small town outside Chicago!

Even though I was scared, I was kind of disappointed, too. I always figured aliens would be real cool-looking. You know, silvery blue skin, huge black eyes, antennae, funky laser guns, stuff like that; I never expected interstellar dweebs.

A Nerd is a Nerd is a Nerd.

Stan rushed across the lawn.

"Greetings from Pan, Agent Mflxnys," said one of the aliens. "May the Crease be with you."

Stan was out there talking to—*a pair of Pants!*

Chapter 8

A NOSE PICKERS' CONVENTION

"Welcome Zgrbnys the Extremely Wise, and Gthrmnys the Utterly Clever," I heard my buddy announce. "How are things on Pan?"

"Oh, just the same old belt loops and cuffs," said Zgrbnys with a shrug.

"The annual Suspender Festival has begun in the Panhandle," put in Gthrmnys. "The Grand Pant himself threw out the first button this year. But enough about home. How have you progressed in your mission?"

"I, Stan, am masquerading as a student in an exchange program," Stan told him. "No one suspects my true identity. I fit right in."

"Oh, sure!" I muttered sarcastically. I could hardly tell him apart from all the other munchkin-sounding, paper-eating, nose-picking dweebs.

"'Stan'?" repeated Gthrmnys in confusion. "What is the meaning of this strange word?"

"It's the name I'm called at my Earthling elementary school," my buddy explained.

The two aliens doubled over with knee-slapping laughter.

"'Stan'!" guffawed Zgrbnys. "Where do Earthlings come up with such ridiculous names?"

"That other one from your last report was even more absurd," chuckled Gthrmnys. "Devin! What kind of a Neptunian Ice Worm would be named Devin?"

I couldn't believe I was being made fun of by a couple of nerds whose names sounded like stomach gurgles. But you can't waste too much time being insulted when your yard is full of aliens.

I had a little trouble eavesdropping on their conversation. The three Pants spoke clearly enough. The problem was they kept picking their noses, so their voices were muffled. It looked like a nose pickers' convention out there!

Life sure can pitch you a lot of curves. One minute you're a normal kid; the next, **you're spying on nose pickers from outer space!**

"I, Stan, have discovered a remarkable Earth device." He handed them my mother's makeup mirror.

I stared. These guys had spaceships, and a *mirror* was a big deal to them?

"It's a truth enforcer," Stan went on. "It's impossible to lie while looking into it."

To demonstrate, he held the mirror in front of their faces. Two sets of alien eyes crossed.

Zgrbnys announced, "I'm much smarter than Gthrmnys."

"Zgrbnys is a moron compared to me," declared Gthrmnys.

Stan took the mirror away, and the two aliens glared at each other resentfully.

Finally, Zgrbnys said, "We must study this baffling object in our laboratory on Pan." Absently, he tossed Mom's mirror over his shoulder. It was about to shatter against the metal of the ship, when a mechanical hand shot out and caught it in midair. Just as suddenly, the mirror was whisked in through the door and out of view.

"What else have you learned about this planet, Agent Mflxnys?" asked Gthrmnys.

"It's very difficult for us Pants to understand Earthlings," Stan told him. "Their main interest seems to be something called 'being cool.' They even have rules about it."

"I had no idea the climate was so important to them," mused Zgrbnys, picking away thoughtfully.

"However, I, Stan, have used my Pan-Tran translator to talk with an Earth-dog named Fungus," Stan went on. "He is a much more sensible life form."

Well, what do you know! Stan wasn't just barking back at Fungus! He could speak *Dog*.

"What forms of entertainment are popular on Earth?" prompted Gthrmnys.

"Scratching, chasing cats, and drinking out of the toilet," Stan replied. "Also, there is something called a fire hydrant. It is so deeply respected that every time you pass one, you must salute it by raising a leg."

"I love native ceremonies," said Zgrbnys approvingly.

"According to Fungus, Earthlings love to bury things," Stan continued. "Especially bones, which are an Earth delicacy."

"How do they taste?" Gthrmnys inquired.

"Not very tender," Stan admitted. "I, Stan, much prefer the flavor of the paper on Earth. It has a nice texture, delicately spiced with ink. The chefs at Sears serve a catalog that is an absolute feast. You must try it."

"Next time," promised Zgrbnys. "Right now, we have an urgent meeting with Agent Shkprnys on Mercury."

Even from my second-story window, I could see my exchange buddy turn pale. "Shkprnys, the One and Only? On Mercury?"

"Don't worry," Gthrmnys assured him. "If your work here goes well, tens of thousands of Pants will be dining on Sears catalogs very, very soon."

What?! Did that mean what I thought it did?

There was only one explanation for so many aliens on Earth. **An invasion! And it was coming *very, very soon!***

After some farewell nose picking, the visitors got back in their ship. First the carpet disappeared. Then the stairs. The big round door shrank and shrank until it was a tiny dot that winked out of existence.

Stan stood there waving as the spacecraft lifted itself off Dad's petunias. It rose up above my window and banked over on its side. Then it hovered for a moment, and zoomed into the night, whizzing around like a balloon with a leak in it. At last, it disappeared.

I didn't move a muscle. I knelt there, frozen, until I heard the back door, and then footsteps in the upstairs hallway. I dove under the covers and faked sleep while Stan let himself into our room.

He got into bed. Almost immediately, I heard the microwave-oven hum of his nose computer.

I opened one eye and peered over at my exchange buddy. Who would have thought that this harmless-looking, nerdy guy was a spy for an invading army? Pretty soon, we Earthlings could be up to our waists in Pants—and not the kind you wear, either.

I set my jaw. I had to stop it. But what could a kid do? Call the police and say, "I'm only nine, but I happen to know the whole planet is about to be attacked by nose pickers from outer space"? They'd throw me in the nuthouse.

I couldn't even tell my parents. I'd just get in trouble for making up stories. It would be that much harder to save the world if I got grounded.

No, I had to do this alone. Stan may have been a highly advanced alien from the other side of the galaxy, but he was still a dweeb. ☞ **Rule 24:** A cool person always has an advantage over a dweeb. I just had to find his weakness.

But what? He had spaceships and technology. He could do just about anything with his nose; I could smell with mine, and that was pretty much it.

What weaknesses did a guy like that have?

The answer would have to come from Stan himself. And I knew the perfect way to squeeze it out of him.

What about Pick-tonyte?

Chapter 9

THE CONSTELLATION OF THE BIG ZIPPER

"Has anybody seen my magnifying mirror?" Mom asked at breakfast the next morning.

I started choking on my Froot Loops. The last I heard, that mirror was on its way to the planet Mercury.

Dad reached over and slapped me on the back.

Roscoe's eyes narrowed. "It was Devin!" he accused. "He was snooping around the bathroom last night while I was in the shower! I'll bet he took it!"

"I did not," I defended myself. It was sort of true. I brought it to my room. But it was Zgrbnys and Gthrmnys who "took" it.

I glanced over at Stan to see if he would rat me out. But the dweeb was barking something at Fungus. He was probably telling him what happened to the mirror, because the two of them shared a pretty good laugh about something.

Mom was annoyed. "Well, please keep an eye out for it," she told us. "It's a very good one. I don't want it to get broken. I'm sure it's just lying around somewhere."

My heart sank. It was lying around somewhere, all right. **Somewhere around the solar system.**

I took Stan to school the back way. My plan was to sneak in before the bell, so I didn't want to run into anyone we knew.

I opened the custodian's entrance, and ushered Stan in ahead of me.

"Where are we going?" he asked.

"I want to show you something cool."

He looked blank. "But I, Stan, am quite comfortable with the temperature."

What a dweeb! I had to remind myself that this was a dangerous alien. The future of the whole world could depend on how I handled him.

I led him to the art room, and peered inside.

Perfect! No teachers in sight. I pulled Stan in after me. Instantly, his eyes crossed.

You see, the art room has a whole wall of mirrors. Mirrors are truth enforcers for Pants. Stan said so himself.

I turned to my exchange buddy. "All right, Mr. Alien, the jig is up! I know everything about you and your nasal processor, and your home planet, and your fellow nose-picking invaders! You're not even a kid, are you? You're 147 years old, just like you said!"

"Incorrect," Stan replied. "My exact age is 146 years, 8 months, 27 days, 12 hours and 16.2 minutes."

Jackpot! He was spilling his guts! "Okay, now you're going to tell me all about Pan."

The crossed eyes blinked. "Pan is a medium-sized planet in the constellation of the Big Zipper. It is roughly eighty-five thousand light-years from Earth."

"Who were those two guys in the backyard last night?" I continued.

"Professional thinkers," said Stan. "On Pan, only our cleverest people are allowed to join the Smarty-Pants."

"You're kidding!" I blurted. **"Smarty-Pants?"**

"The Smarty-Pants can think in six dimensions," he informed me. "They can answer a question even before it's asked; they can program any VCR in the galaxy. They know the meaning of life, the capital of the Crab Nebula, and why manhole covers are round. Their IQs are so large that even *they* can't count that high. They are the most important citizens of Pan, except for the Grand Pant himself, and his assistants, the Under-Pants."

What *was* this, a comedy routine? Smarty-Pants, Under-Pants, the Big Zipper—

"I suppose there's a T-shirt planet somewhere," I said sarcastically. **"In the constellation of the Short Sleeve."**

Stan's eyes never uncrossed. "I know of no such place."

I had to quit fooling around. This could be a matter of life and death. Earth was in danger.

"When is the invasion going to start?" I demanded.

He looked blank. "What invasion?"

"Don't try to deny it!" I pushed him right up to the mirror. His eyes got so crossed I thought they'd roll down his cheeks.

"But Pan is a peaceful planet," he told me.

"We don't even have an army."

"That's just what a spy would say," I accused. "Right, *Agent* Mflxnys?"

"I, Stan, am not that kind of agent," he insisted.

"Oh, yeah? What kind of agent are you, then?"

"A travel agent," he announced.

I was thunderstruck. "A *travel agent*? But—that's impossible! I heard those Smarty-Pants guys talking about your people swarming all over Earth!"

"Yes," Stan agreed. "Tourists. We Pants are the greatest tourists in the galaxy. We work two weeks per year and go on vacation for the other fifty. I, Stan, am in charge of all the test tourists here on Earth."

"What are test tourists?" I asked suspiciously.

"Pants like me," he explained. "They pose as humans. But they're really doing research to see if Earth can become Pan's newest vacation resort. I, Stan, use my nasal processor to beam our findings to the Smarty-Pants. The Smarty-Pants report to the Under-Pants, who make a

presentation to the Grand Pant himself. It's all very top drawer."

I let my breath out in a long sigh of relief. "Oh, phew! I was freaking out! I thought we were going to have a whole nose-picking army attacking us from spaceships!" I was so happy I actually hugged him. I know Rule 8 says: ☞ **No hugging,** but I was pretty emotional. "I don't care if you're an alien. I'm just glad Earth isn't in danger."

"There *is* one small problem," Stan admitted. "After scouring a hundred and fourteen planets in fifty-three star systems, the Smarty-Pants have narrowed the choices down to two final-ists—Earth and Mercury."

"Mercury?" I repeated. "Who'd want to go *there*?"

"I, Stan, agree. It's not the humidity. It's the heat. But the travel agent on Mercury is—" He gulped. "Shkprnys, the One and Only."

I frowned. "Who's Shkprnys?"

"Only the greatest agent in the history of the Pan-Pan Travel Bureau," Stan said in awed respect. "It was his idea to build the Red Spot Amusement Park on Jupiter. He made meteor surfing the fastest growing sport in the galaxy. He was the one who told the owner of the Little Dipper, **'We could use another of those, but next time make it *big*.'**"

"Well, if he's so good at his job," I reasoned, "he's bound to see that Earth is the better planet."

Stan shook his head. "A long time ago, when Shkprnys was a Training Pant, he was sent on a mission to Earth. Wouldn't you know it? He got very itchy poison ivy. His ship ran out of calamine lotion near Halley's Comet, and he scratched for seventy thousand light-years. He's had a grudge against Earth ever since."

I shrugged. "So we lose. Let Mercury have all the tourists. Who needs the extra traffic, anyway?"

"You don't understand," Stan insisted. "Mercury has a spectacular view of the rings of Saturn. But there's something in the way."

"What?" I asked.

"Earth. So it would have to be moved, of course."

I was shocked. *"Moved?* Where?"

"Somewhere out past the orbit of Pluto," admitted Stan.

"Past *Pluto*?" I cried. "But—that's too far from the Sun! We'll all freeze!"

"The Pan-Pan Travel Bureau realizes this would condemn Earth to a frosty future." It was Stan's turn to shrug. "But we Pants take vacationing very seriously, and a view is a view, and—" He looked horribly distressed. "I, Stan, am most sincerely sorry, Devin."

Before I could react, there was a commotion

outside in the hall.

"Let me through!" shouted someone.

I went to the door—and nearly got trampled.

"Stand aside in the name of planetary defense!" the voice bellowed right in my ear.

It was Mr. Slomin!

Chapter 10
DOING SOMETHING COOL

The teacher was red-faced and wild-eyed—the way he always looked when he was on a UFO hunt. UFOs! Aliens! Who ever thought Mr. Slomin would turn out to be right about that stuff?

He must have sprinted all the way from his car, because he was huffing and puffing.

"I've got proof!" he wheezed, waving a roll of film. "Proof that aliens visit Earth! Last night I took pictures of a UFO landing right near your house, Devin! Did you see anything?"

"No," I replied quickly.

"Yes," said Stan.

I totally forgot that we were still in front of the mirror. Stan *had* to tell the truth. He had no choice!

He started to spill the beans. "Your 'UFO' is a space cruiser of the first fleet of his most tailored majesty, the Grand—"

I slapped my hand over his mouth. If Mr. Slomin found out about Stan, he might turn him in to the Air Force. Remember what happened to E. T.? And Stan was the travel agent in charge of Earth! Without him—*whoosh!* Out past Pluto.

I pushed him out of the art room hard enough to put him through the hallway wall. His eyes uncrossed as he slid down to the floor, dazed.

Mr. Slomin rushed into the photography darkroom. "I've got to develop this film right away!" He slammed the door shut behind him.

This was all I needed—pictures of Stan and his two weirdo friends, standing by their spaceship

with their fingers up their noses. It would be on the the front page of every newspaper in the world!

* EXTRA! EXTRA! *
READ ALL ABOUT IT:
Aliens pick their noses, too!

I had to destroy that film! I counted to three, took a deep breath, and yanked the door open.

"*Aaaaaaaaaaah!!*"

There was Mr. Slomin, with the film stretched out like a ribbon in front of him. Even in the dim light, I could see his face changing color—first to red, then to purple.

"It's *ruined!*" he howled. "The only proof the UFO Society ever had! Devin, don't you know film gets spoiled if you expose it to light?"

"Sorry," I mumbled.

"You're on detention for this!" he roared. "A *month* of detentions! No, a *year*!"

"But Mr. Slomin," came a voice from the hall, "I, Stan, am the one to blame."

"What?" Mr. Slomin stormed out of the darkroom and turned burning eyes on my exchange buddy. "Explain yourself!"

"I, Stan, made Devin ruin your film," Stan told the teacher. "I—dared him to open the door."

I couldn't believe it! Stan was trying to get me off the hook!

Taking the rap to help a friend—that was . . . that was . . .

Why, that was Rule 17!

S t a n   M f l x n y s,   nose-picking   paper-eating,   alien-dweeb   travel   agent,   was   doing   something *cool!*

Chapter 11

I WILL NOT RUIN ANY MORE PICTURES OF UFOS

Mr. Slomin developed his film anyway, but the results were—hooray!—very bad. There were no pictures. Only a long strip of blank negatives remained from his night of UFO-spotting.

He was a one-man thunderstorm, lightning bolts and all.

"You're *both* on double-detention!" he roared at us. "Now, get to class! The bell's about to ring!"

As we hurried through the halls, I whispered, "Thanks—"

"*Silence!*" thundered Mr. Slomin.

All day, Stan and I sat side by side under our teacher's furious glare.

Didn't it figure? For the first time, I really

wanted to talk to Stan. There was so much I needed to say. But if Mr. Slomin heard even the slightest little peep coming from either of us today, we were both dead meat.

Even at recess, I didn't get a chance to speak with the guy—not with all the nose-picking jokes and half the class dancing around singing, **"I, Stan, Stan the Man, Stan from Pan, the Panty Man!"**

One thing was different this time. I sure wasn't going to let those jerks get away with making fun of *my* exchange buddy.

"Hey, shut up!" I snapped. "Leave him alone!"

At lunch, when Stan ate his cardboard chocolate milk container, Calista tried to make a big deal about it.

"Ooh, gross! Look, everybody! That's totally disgusting!"

I fixed her. "Poor Stan," I whispered. "He suffers from a rare vitamin deficiency. That's why he eats paper. Because he needs more vitamin P."

I made her feel so guilty she was almost in tears. She even gave him her lunch bag for dessert.

"Take out your writing journals," announced Mr. Slomin when we got back to class. "Today's topic is UFOs."

Calista raised her hand. "Mr. Slomin, the newspaper said that there are *no* UFOs. The sighting at the airport last week was all a big mistake."

"Then why did the same spaceship come back last night?" challenged the teacher.

"Really?" breathed Wanda.

"I have proof—" The teacher glared at Stan and me. "I mean, I *had* proof. The government doesn't want us to know that alien races visit us. At my last UFO Society meeting, we figured out that the first spacecraft got close enough to the airport to drop a package into the baggage system."

A package named Stan! Uh-oh. Those UFO Society guys were pretty sharp. I had to throw Mr. Slomin off the scent!

I opened my journal and wrote: *There are plenty of "flying objects" at the airport, and none of them are unidentified. They're called planes.*

That was no good. Mr. Slomin would get mad and flunk me!

Suddenly, a loud whisper came from Tanner. **"Steam shovel!"**

Steam shovel was Class 4C's new code word. It meant that Stan was "picking" his nose again. The joke was that his finger was like the digging arm of a big power shovel. Of course, I knew it wasn't *real* picking. What was Stan up to?

I looked down. My journal entry was erasing itself like the ink was being lifted clear off the paper! Then, to my amazement, a full-page essay appeared. It was even in my handwriting!

It was Stan! He knew I was getting myself in trouble, and he was using his nose computer to save me from Mr. Slomin. But with the teacher watching us like a hawk, I couldn't even say thanks.

What a day! When it was finally 3:30, we still had our double detention to live through. Mr. Slomin made us write two hundred lines each: *I will not ruin any more pictures of UFOs.* Worst of all, he sat there staring at us the whole time. So Stan couldn't even use his nose computer to do the work for us.

At last, when the hour was over, we scram-

bled out of the school like we were being released from prison. We ran all the way home. On
the porch, I leaned on Stan as the two of us
caught our breath.

"Thanks for saving me in journal-writing," I
panted. "It was a really cool thing to do."

"Cool?" Stan was confused. "My nasal
processor has indicated normal temperatures all
day."

"Listen, Stan," I explained patiently. "I don't mean cool like *cold*. I mean cool like *hip—happening—sweet—awesome*!"

Up went the steam shovel finger again. Stan seemed even more bewildered. "My computer does not recognize these words the way you are using them." He frowned. "How can I, Stan, be a travel agent on Earth if I barely understand the place myself?"

"I'll tell you everything you need to know," I assured him. "But you've got to promise that you won't let them move us out past Pluto! I can barely stand the winter in *this* orbit! I hate shoveling snow!"

"I, Stan, will do my best," Stan said sincerely. "But I don't stand a chance against Shkprnys, the One and Only. Why would the Grand Pant listen to me instead of a travel agent who could fill a Roach Motel in hyperspace? Shkprnys is a legend, and I—" He shrugged. "—I, Stan, am just a kid."

"Just a kid?" I echoed. "I thought you were 147 years old."

"That *is* a kid," he told me. "On Pan, the voting age is 250. Shkprnys is well over five hundred."

"I'll tell you what," I offered, ushering him in through the door. "Tonight I'll put all my rules of coolness on flash cards. When I get through with you, you'll be Pan's number one Earth expert. Then the Grand Pant will have to pay attention to you."

He seemed worried. "Being cool is extremely complicated. Even the Smarty-Pants don't understand it. And they know why manhole covers are round."

"Don't sweat it," I said. "I wrote the book on coolness. If anyone can help you, I can."

"Stan, is that you?" called Roscoe from the den. "I taped yesterday's Bulls game. Come on, let's watch it!"

Stan looked at me. "Would this be a cool thing to do?"

I nodded. "Very cool."

We plopped ourselves down on the couch beside Roscoe. Chicago had a 29–27 lead early in the second quarter.

Michael Jordan was handling the ball. Suddenly, he blew past the defense, leaped high in the air, and executed an unbelievable reverse slam dunk—I gawked—*all with his finger up his nose!*

I wheeled to face Stan. "*Michael Jordan* is an *alien?*" I whispered incredulously.

He shrugged. "You didn't think a mere Earthling could jam like that, did you?"

Chapter 12

DUMMY PANTS

Maybe it was the idea that Michael Jordan was one of the test tourists, and Stan was his boss. But I started to have a lot more respect for my exchange buddy.

We made a pretty good team. I gave him great things about Earth to tell the Smarty-Pants. And he used his nose computer to help me with chores around the house.

You know how fast Stan took care of the dishes? Well, his nasal processor could make a bed in half that time. Cleaning my room took less than a second. With the flick of that steam shovel finger, all our stuff would be back in its place. The carpet would even be vacuumed.

I'VE GOT TO GET ME ONE OF THOSE.

"This is better than maid service," I chortled, checking out our perfect closet. "Hey, what happened to your Michael Jordan shirt?"

"Oh, Mchlnys needed it back," he replied. "There was a laundry strike at the United Center. All his jerseys were sweaty, and mine was the only clean one on Earth."

That weekend, Mom put me in charge of cleaning out the garage.

"You'd better start warming up your schnoz," I advised. "Our garage is a disaster area, no lie."

He just smiled sweetly and stuck his finger up his nose. Three seconds later, he was done.

"Not possible!" I exclaimed. "Cleaning that garage takes two days! We've got lawn chairs, and gardening stuff, and sports equipment, and old shoes, and tools! And it all has to be hosed down! And then put back!"

"The task is complete," Stan assured me.

So I took his word for it. We went back to work on his report to the Smarty-Pants.

About an hour later, Mom appeared in the doorway. She was bug-eyed. "Devin, I don't know what to say."

My first thought was that Stan's nasal processor had trashed the garage.

"I—I didn't do it!" I blurted.

She threw her arms around me and kissed my cheek. "Of course you did it. I've never seen the garage looking better!"

"Uh—Stan helped," I managed.

She hugged him, too. "I can't believe how much work you did. All that cleaning, putting up

those new shelves for the paint cans—and how did you ever untangle that snarl of hoses? Your father and I have been trying for years!"

"It went fast," I told her with a wink at Stan.

"You didn't happen to see my makeup mirror out there, did you?" she asked, shaking her head. "It's still missing."

"Sorry, Mom," I mumbled. And when she was gone, I turned to my exchange buddy. "Hey, when are those Smarty-Pants guys coming back with Mom's mirror?"

Stan shuffled uncomfortably. "There's been a little accident."

"They broke it?" I asked.

"No," he assured me, "it's in one piece. But that piece was ejected out the trash chute of their ship." He looked sheepish. "It disappeared down the black hole of Cygnus X-1."

"What?" I was horrified. "I thought they were supposed to be Smarty-Pants! **They sound like a couple of Dummy Pants to me!"**

"It could happen to anybody," Stan defended his fellow Pants. "Black holes are hard to spot in deep space. They're very dark."

"But that's an expensive mirror," I complained. "Can't they fly into the black hole and get it?"

"Oh, no," Stan said seriously. "Nothing can escape the pull of a black hole. Not even light. If they fly in, they could never fly out. They'd be sucked down."

"Would they die?" I asked.

Stan shrugged. "Nobody knows. No one has ever flown into a black hole. One theory is that the black hole spits you out somewhere. But it could be anywhere in the universe. You might end up a hundred billion light-years away in a distant galaxy. Even the Smarty-Pants aren't sure."

Oh, great. Mom always wanted to travel. Well, she was stuck at home, but her mirror sure was getting the grand tour. "At least they didn't break it," I mumbled.

Suddenly, Stan sprang to his feet and put his finger up his nose.

I eyed him suspiciously. "Listen, Stan. I'm taking your word for it that the nose picking is for official business. If you're sneaking in a few extra picks—"

"This is urgent!" he interrupted me. "My nasal

processor has intercepted a message to the Smarty-Pants. It's Shkprnys's latest report on Mercury."

"What does it say?" I asked.

Stan ran to the computer on my desk. He yanked out the printer cable and stuck the loose end up his nose. The operating lights went crazy, blinking brighter and faster than ever before.

"Ugh," I grimaced. "You expect me to use that after it's been up your schnoz?"

A single page printed. I stared at the message from another world.

Chapter 13

MESSAGE FROM MERCURY

∗∗∗ PANT-O-GRAM ∗∗∗

TO: *Smarty-Pants Main Thinking Center*
FROM: *Shkprnys, the One and Only*

Forsooth, Mercury hath great warmth
to sun thy buns . . .

I looked up from the paper. "What language is this?"

"Oh, it's English," Stan chuckled. "Remember, Shkprnys left Earth four hundred years ago. That's how people talked back then."

I snorted. "Who does he think he is? Shakespeare?"

84

"Yes," Stan replied.

"*What?!*"

He looked at me earnestly. "You didn't think a mere Earthling could write like that, did you?"

"Shakespeare? *William* Shakespeare? But he's dead! He died hundreds of years ago!"

Stan shook his head. "Shakespeare didn't die. He just got poison ivy. That's the only reason he left Earth."

I was bug-eyed. "Are you telling me that **Romeo and Juliet was written by a travel agent?**"

"Well, he wasn't a travel agent yet," Stan explained. "He was still a Training Pant. Kind of like kindergarten here on Earth. It was fine for Shkprnys to scribble his little plays back then. But it's no career for an adult."

"So to get the Grand Pant to pick Earth over Mercury," I said slowly, "we're going to have to write a better paper than *Shakespeare*?"

"I, Stan, told you it was a long shot."

"Man, we'd better get busy!" I turned back to the report we'd been working on.

Great Tourist Attractions of Earth

DEVIN'S LIST

- video games
- Disney World
- comic books
- the Grand Canyon
- MTV
- Hawaii
- waterskiing

STAN'S LIST

- dog humor
- mirrors
- traffic jams
- going to the dentist
- delicious paper
- homework
- allergies

I stared at him. "You expect to beat Shakespeare with *this*? People *hate* traffic jams and homework! And what's so great about allergies?"

"Smarty-Pants scientists have eliminated dust and mold and ragweed," Stan explained.

"So there are no allergies on Pan."

"That's good," I began. "Isn't it?"

"For us Pants, sneezing is the most wonderfully entertaining activity there is," he informed me. "There's no feeling quite like a nostril-busting blast of wind shooting through a supercomputer. Every single one of your trillion gigabytes tingles." He turned tragic. "At least, that's what I've heard. The last Pant to sneeze was Nfrgnys the Snuffler way back in 1745."

Maybe it was all this allergy talk, but a little dust got up my nose. "A-*choo!*"

"That looked like fun," said Stan wistfully.

"Maybe it's better when you have a computer up there," I admitted.

"I, Stan, believe that Pants will flock to Earth for a chance to be allergic again."

"You mean," I said incredulously, "that you expect people to travel eighty-five thousand light-years just to sneeze?"

Stan looked annoyed. "I, Stan, invite you to come up with something better."

It takes all kinds to make a galaxy . . .

"Everything on my list is better than sneezing," I argued. "Like waterskiing. What could be more exciting than zooming across the lake behind a speedboat? Wiping out, and swimming to shore—"

"Swimming?" Stan put his finger up his nose. "My nasal processor does not recognize this word."

I was horrified. "You mean you can't swim?"

The steam shovel finger probed a little deeper. "My computer has searched every book in every library on Pan," Stan reported. "At no time on record has any Pant performed this 'swimming.'"

"But we've got fourth-grade field day coming up on Monday!" I cried. "The swimming race is the most important event!"

"Perhaps I, Stan, should not participate in field day."

"Oh, you're participating," I assured him. "All *three* of us are."

The fried-egg eyes looked confused. "All three of us?"

"Right," I told him. **"You, me, and your magic nose!"**

Chapter 14

ZAP!

"What perfect weather for field day!" exclaimed Mr. Slomin. "Blue skies with just a hint of winter around the corner!"

Soccer Sam was showing Tanner how to keep a ball in the air using only his knees and chest. I have to admit Tanner was getting pretty good.

"Hey, Devin, look at this!" he called to me. "That field day trophy is as good as ours!"

"I don't know about that," I said slyly. "You're up against some pretty tough teams."

"Like who?" challenged Sam.

"Like—" I smiled sweetly, "—me and Stan."

Tanner laughed so hard that he lost control of the ball. "You and *Stan*? You guys don't have a prayer—not unless nose picking is a new event this year!"

I just kept on smiling. And guess who turned
out to be our opponents for the very first event?
Tanner and Sam.

It was two-on-two soccer. Tanner and I were
the goalies.

Sam stole the ball and danced around Stan.
My teammate offered about as much defense as
a mailbox. He just stood there while Sam took a
booming kick.

And then Stan put his finger up his nose.

It happened so fast you could barely see it. The ball hurtled toward the open side of the net. Suddenly, Stan zipped out in front of it, and— *pow!*—he headed the ball so hard that it took off like a rocket. It flew clear across the field. Tanner dove for it, but he had no chance. 1–0.

"What a play!" cried Mr. Slomin. "Stan, how did you do that?"

"He, Stan, has been practic-
ing," I supplied smugly.

Stan scored four more goals, and we skunked
them 5–0. Stan also starred in the volleyball
game, the egg-and-spoon race, the beanbag toss,
the obstacle course, and the pogo-stick competi-
tion. He won all the track-and-field events by a
nose—if you know what I mean.

I was his partner in the three-legged race. He went so fast that I felt like I was being pulled alongside a speeding car.

By the time Mr. Slomin led us over to the high school's indoor pool, we had won every single event. Only the swimming relay stood between us and the field day championship.

While we were changing into bathing suits, I noticed Stan was looking really pale. I gave him a friendly nudge. "Don't worry if you're not such a terrific swimmer."

"That's not it," he said nervously. "I, Stan, have intercepted another message from Shakespeare. He has completed Mercury's official tourist slogan. We have to respond with a slogan for Earth!"

"Not now!" I insisted, tying a string to the ear-pieces of his glasses. I plopped them back on his nose and marched him out to the pool. "We're in first place by a mile. We would have to finish dead last in this race to lose the trophy."

He gaped. "You mean swimming happens in *there*?" he asked, pointing. "In *water*?"

"You go first, and I'm next," I coached. "Just—you know—follow your nose."

"On your marks," announced Mr. Slomin. "Get set—"

"But Devin," he whined, "I, Stan, cannot—"

The teacher blew his whistle. "Go!"

The other kids dove in. Stan didn't budge.

"Go!" I hissed.

"But—"

What could I do? I reached out and shoved him over the side.

Stan belly flopped into the pool like a thousand-pound bag of cement. His head went under, and he breathed in a huge snootful of water.

ZAP!

A lightning bolt shot out of his nose. When he came up again, his nostrils were shooting sparks. Smoke puffed out of his ears.

"Your schnoz!" I shouted. "Use your schnoz!"

He reached in with a finger. Nothing happened.

"Keep trying!" I yowled.

But Stan was already sinking to the bottom of the pool in a shower of frothy bubbles. I had to jump in there and rescue him.

When I finally hauled him out, he smelled like burning machinery. His ears smoldered.

Wanda won the first lap, with Cody hot on her heels. Their buddies, Calista and Joey, dove in.

Remember how we'd have to finish dead last to lose the trophy? Well, scratch that. Not finishing at all gets you disqualified. **Almost drowning gets you laughed at.**

Calista hit the finish line amid a roar of cheers.

I'll bet I was smoking worse than Stan when Mr. Slomin added up the field day final results.

"First place, Calista and Wanda; second place, Tanner and Sam; third place, Joey and Cody . . ."

It went on for a pretty long time, but he finally got to us. "Last place, Devin and Stan. Too bad, fellows. You were winning until the very end."

I turned on my exchange buddy. "What happened?"

He pulled up his glasses which were over his mouth. The fried-egg eyes looked haunted. "My nasal processor must never come in contact with H_2O!"

Uh-oh. "You mean—"

He nodded miserably. "I, Stan," he announced in a watery munchkin voice, "have short-circuited my nose."

Chapter 15
THE PANIC BUTTON

I cleaned my room the old-fashioned way that afternoon. It was torture. I had to pick up every single comic book, chess piece, Magic Marker, and every dollar of Monopoly money *myself*!

You never appreciate what you have until it's gone.

"Try your nose again," I said to Stan.

He reached up there, but it was no use. He may as well have been picking it for real.

CrY ME a riVer.

"Nothing," he mourned. "I, Stan, have shorted out the central processing control. We Pants call it the Panic Button."

"Well, this stinks," I mumbled. "So much for maid service."

"It's more serious than that, Devin," Stan said in agitation. "The Smarty-Pants received Shake-speare's slogan at three o'clock. It was a smash hit."

"That good, huh?"

He nodded. "*'To tan or not to tan. That is the question on Mercury.'*"

I frowned. "What's so great about that?"

"It's brilliant!" cried Stan. "Half of Mercury is always facing the sun. The other half is always in the dark. So, depending on whether or not you want a tan, that's the side of the planet you go to."

"That's the best Shakespeare can do?" I asked.

"It's much better than the old slogan," Stan informed me. "*'Come to Mercury. It's like a sauna out here.'*"

"This is the best news I've heard all day," I promised Stan. "Shakespeare's slogan stinks. I'll bet we can come up with something about Earth that blows away *'To tan or not to tan.'*"

Stan looked distressed. "But how could I, Stan, send our slogan to Pan? My nasal processor won't work without a new Panic Button. That's the only way to get a message home."

I shrugged. "Can't the Smarty-Pants fix it?"

"The Smarty-Pants can fix anything, of course," he said. "But Zgrbnys and Gthrmnys might not come here for another month. Now that Mercury's slogan is in, the clock starts ticking. I, Stan, have exactly one week and one hour to respond. Otherwise Mercury gets chosen automatically. And that means—"

I finished the sentence. "*Whoosh!* Out past Pluto." I thought fast. "Hey, what about some of the other Pants living on Earth? You know, the test tourists, like Michael Jordan. Couldn't he get you a new part?"

He shook his head. "The Panic Button is advanced Smarty-Pants technology. Most ordinary Pants wouldn't have it. And their nasal processors wouldn't be strong enough to communicate with Pan directly. Except—" He looked thoughtful. "There is one test tourist in California who used to be a Smarty-Pant. He quit to join the artistic union—the Tights and Tutus."

"This guy isn't another five-hundred-year-old playwright, is he?" I said suspiciously. "Or is he just in the NBA?"

"Neither," said Stan. "His name is Lnrdnys. But here on Earth he's known as Leonardo Di-Caprio."

"Leonardo DiCaprio?" I echoed. **"The *movie star?*"**

Stan shrugged. "You didn't think a mere Earthling could act like that, did you?"

I grabbed Stan's arm. "Let's go call him."

"We communicate by nose," he informed me.

SO, whY didN'T hE USE his NOSE COMPUTEr tO UNSiNK thE TitaNic?

"I, Stan, do not have his phone number. We'll have to reach him by mail."

"By mail?" I was horrified. "Are you crazy? Movie stars get a million letters a day! What makes you think he'll read ours?"

"He reads them all," said Stan.

"How do you know?"

"Lnrdnys has a very large appetite," he explained. "He's a growing boy of only 120. He

101

eats all his fan mail—but he reads it first."

He took a piece of paper out of my desk and nibbled at the corner. "Mmm. Tasty."

"Don't eat Leonardo DiCaprio's letter," I said sternly. "We want to put him in a good mood. Hey, if he and Michael Jordan are both Pants, how come they're cool-looking, and you and those Smarty-Pants guys dress like meganerds?"

"Lnrdnys and Mchlnys have been on Earth too long," Stan explained as he wrote. "When you run out of high-fashion white shirts and polka-dot ties, you have to settle for Earth clothes."

I peered over Stan's shoulder at the paper.

Dear Lnrdnys the Ravenously Hungry,

I am off-line. Please send me one replacement Panic Button.
Extremely urgent!

Yours truly,
Agent Mflxnys (Stan)
Pan-Pan Travel Bureau

PS: Loved you in <u>Titanic</u>.
PPS: May the Crease be with you!

"Hey, Stan," I asked while he addressed the envelope, "what's this Crease you Pants are always talking about?"

"There's a Crease in the fabric of the universe," he explained. "An endless amount of energy flows through it. That's where we Pants get the power for our spaceships, our nasal processors, and everything on Pan."

Fungus came along with us to the mailbox. The two of them were barking the whole way. I felt kind of left out.

"What's he saying?" I asked.

"Fungus is a big Leonardo DiCaprio fan," Stan translated.

"Yeah, well, so is Lindsay," I warned. "Don't tell her you know the guy, or we'll never hear the end of it."

Stan opened the mailbox and dropped the letter inside. Suddenly, he covered his face. "A-*choo!*"

When he took away his hands, he was grinning from ear to ear. "That was fantastic! I, Stan, have experienced sneezation!"

"Gesundheit," I said sarcastically.

"Do you suppose that I, Stan, might be allergic to something?"

"You're probably just getting a cold," I replied. "You know, from your dunk in the pool today."

"A cold? A *cold?*" I'd never seen anybody so happy. "Allergies, perhaps, but I never dreamed I would be lucky enough to catch a cold!"

He practically danced all the way home. Fun-

gus and I had to run to keep up with him. When we rounded the corner, we found the whole family standing outside. They were gathered around the big tree in our front yard. It was lying flat on the grass beside a gigantic hole in the lawn.

"What happened to the tree?" I asked.

Dad shook his head, bewildered. "I can't explain it! One minute it was standing there. Then it just . . . popped out, roots and all!"

Lindsay was crying. "But what would make a whole tree jump out of the ground?"

We could only exchange baffled looks.

Chapter 16

A FLYING ROLL OF
TOILET PAPER

With the letter on its way to Leonardo Di-Caprio, we set to work on a tourist slogan for Earth. When the new Panic Button arrived, and Stan could fix his nose, we had to be ready with something at least as good as *"To tan or not to tan."*

Every day after school, we held a brainstorming session. Every night, before falling asleep, we tossed ideas around. But by Saturday morning, all we had was:

DEVIN'S LIST
- *Earth: It's A World of Fun*
- *Mmm, Mmm, Earth*

- Go, Big Blue
- Mercury Bites

STAN'S LIST
- Come to the 847th Cleanest
  Planet in the Galaxy
- Pigeon Capital of the Cosmos
- Free Oxygen

"It's no use," said my exchange buddy. "I, Stan, have writer's block."

"Me, too," I admitted. "Man, I'll bet Shakespeare never gets writer's block."

"That's why he's 'The One and Only,'" Stan sighed. "While I, Stan, have no title. I'm just—Mflxnys. Mflxnys the—" He shook his head. "Nothing."

But I wasn't going to lie down and die like Stan. It wasn't *his* planet that was heading for the deep freeze. I practically dragged him to the bus stop. How does an alien travel agent learn about Earth? From an *Earth* travel agent!

The local transit pulled up, and its doors folded open. Stan and I got in line behind the other passengers. They each paid their fare. Then it was Stan's turn. He stuck his nose into the coin box and snorted.

TALK about dirty MONEY!

I thought the driver was going to have a heart attack. "That's disgusting! What are you—a pig?"

Quickly, I paid for both of us and hustled Stan to an empty seat. He was really sorry for doing

such a dumb thing. "That was my mistake. I, Stan, should have remembered that my nasal processor is on the fritz."

"You're not thinking," I said crossly. "On Earth we pay with our money, not our noses."

"We tried money on Pan, but it was a disaster," he explained. "Pants can't resist paper. People ate their life savings. Lnrdnys devoured almost fifty-thousand pantaloons and had to go to the hospital with severe indigestion. He barely had enough cash left to pay his doctor bill. So now checking, credit cards, even mutual funds are in our computers, hooked into the planetary bank, the Pocket." He looked sad. "When my Panic Button shorted out, my accounts all reset to zero."

He lifted a Kleenex to his face. I thought he was going to cry, but instead—

"A-*choo!*"

This was the fifth day of his cold, and he was loving every minute of it. He refused to take any medicine. He wouldn't even eat chicken soup. My mother thought his appetite was suffering, but I knew the real reason. He didn't want to get better. For him, "sneezation" was a barrel of laughs.

Suddenly, the driver slammed on the brakes. "What the—" A telephone pole had fallen across the road, blocking our lane. The bus screeched to a halt two inches in front of it.

I looked out the window as we drove around it. "The wind?" I said dubiously.

But nothing could take Stan's mind off the joy of sneezing. He grinned all the way downtown.

The driver was still mad at Stan when we got off. "Hey, kid. From now on, keep your nose to yourself."

"A-*choo!*" Stan replied with a wave of apology.

There was a commotion on the street. Something was wrong with the fountain in front of Clearview Travel. Instead of water, a thick pink liquid was bubbling out of the spout.

A little kid stuck his face in the middle of it and took a taste. "It's milk shake!" he cried in delight. "Strawberry milk shake!"

"Fascinating," commented Stan. "Milk shakes occur in nature, like oil gushers and hot springs."

"No, they don't!" I snapped, shoving him

ahead of me through the revolving door into the travel agency. "A lot of weird stuff has been happening, but it's not normal. Now pay attention. We're here to get slogan ideas."

I picked up a handful of vacation brochures and fanned them like playing cards under his nose. "Check this out: Paradise Island, Bahamas. White sand, blue water, sun, surf—"

I could see Stan wasn't very impressed.

"Water, Devin. We Pants have to avoid it. The Pan-Pan Travel Bureau wouldn't be too pleased with spaceship-loads of dissatisfied customers, with their Panic Buttons fried, and their savings reset to zero."

"Well, how about this, then?" I persisted. "Snowboarding in the Canadian Rockies. What a vacation!"

"Humdrum," Stan yawned. "We're looking for scenery, atmosphere, wildlife."

The manager came over. "Can I help you boys find something?"

"Oh, yes, please," said Stan. "Do you know of any place dark and damp with plenty of insects?"

The man gave him a strained smile. "How about my basement?"

"What he means," I explained quickly, "is we're looking for somewhere—you know—bad."

I could see that he wanted to throw us out. So I added, "It's for a school project." Adults will do almost anything if they think they're helping education.

So he dug up an ancient cobweb-covered file marked UNUSUAL DESTINATIONS. The top folder was entitled SIBERIA WINTER CARNIVAL.

I didn't get to see much more because a puff of dust from the old papers went up Stan's nose.

"A-choo!"

There were screams from the washroom at the back of the office. The door burst open, and out ran a terrified lady. **She was being chased by a flying roll of toilet paper.** It caught up with her near the water cooler, wrapped her from head to toe like a mummy, and then took off after the manager.

In that instant, everything became clear. I wheeled to face my exchange buddy. "It's *you*!" I rasped.

"Me?" snuffled Stan.

"Every time you sneeze, something crazy happens! Remember? You sneezed at the mailbox right before our tree popped out! *And* when the pole fell over! *And* when the fountain started spitting up milk shake!"

Stan considered this. "It *is* logical. My nasal processor is powered by the Crease. But because my nose has a short circuit, huge amounts of loose energy are released by each sneeze."

"What can we do to stop it?" I hissed.

Stan looked noble. "I, Stan, must immediately cease sneezation—a-*choo*!"

The whole office tilted over on its side. Big desks and computers went crashing into the wall that was now the floor. The carpet flapped, releasing a blizzard of dust.

"Hold your breath!" I yowled at Stan.

But he'd already inhaled a cloud of the stuff. "A-*choo!* A-*choo!* A-*choo!* A-*choo!* . . ."

Now the furniture was airborne. A cement truck drove through the front window and rear-ended a filing cabinet. Milk shake from the foun-tain oozed in through the broken glass, soaking the papers that lay everywhere. Plane tickets and schedules turned to mush.

☛ **Rule 31:** Always get out of there before anybody has a chance to figure out it's all your fault.

I grabbed Stan by the arm, and we started climbing toward the revolving door.

Chapter 17

SOMETHING WEIRD
IS GOING ON

Every Monday at three, Mr. Slomin taught Current Events. Each student got a copy of the *Clearview Post*. I took one look at the headline and almost swallowed my tongue.

SOMETHING WEIRD IS GOING ON!

Scientists still can't explain what turned Clearview Travel into a demolition derby last Saturday. But even stranger things have been happening around town since then.

What could make a seventy-foot dandelion grow in front of City Hall in a single night? Did the water tower really tap-dance on its support beams? How come the Clearview Copper Mine is producing goat cheese? What changed all the toilet seats at police headquarters into rosebushes? No one really knows. . . .

"We're dead!" I whispered to Stan. "If any-body finds out that *your nose* is the cause of it all, they'll throw us in jail! Or worse, they'll make us clean it up! How'd you like to be sent over to Clearview Travel with a broom?"

Even Stan had come to realize that sneezing wasn't such a great thing after all. "This is no time for jokes, Devin. It's exactly one week since Shakespeare submitted his dazzling slogan, *'To tan or not to tan.'* There's only one hour left before—"

"*Whoosh,*" I finished glumly. "Out past Pluto."

"We have no slogan," Stan went on. "And even if we did, we have no way to communicate with the Smarty-Pants."

"Where's Leonardo DiCaprio with our new Panic Button?" I demanded.

"I, Stan, hope he didn't eat my letter before reading it."

I was horrified. "Could that happen?"

"If he was having an extra-hungry day," Stan admitted.

Well, that was reassuring. I was ten times more worried now.

"Quiet, everyone," ordered Mr. Slomin. "I want to finish Current Events before it's time to go home. Now, who would like to comment on the article?"

Wanda raised her hand. "I think it's scary."

"But kind of funny, too," added Joey. "You know, the part where the chief of police had to go to the hospital to get the thorns pulled out."

A lot of kids laughed, but not Stan or me.

"It's not funny *or* scary," the teacher told us. "It's *suspicious*. It's no accident that these strange events are happening right after two UFO sightings. This is the work of aliens—*Stan*!"

I almost jumped out of my skin. **Did Mr. Slomin *know?***

"Stan, I gave you those tissues for your cold," the teacher said crossly. "Stop eating them."

"Sorry, Mr. Slomin." But as soon as Stan took the tissue away from his face, he sneezed.

The venetian blinds on our windows clattered up and down three times.

Nervous laughter buzzed through the room. Mr. Slomin frowned.

"A-*choo*!" Stan sneezed again.

The teacher's heavy desk launched itself up off the floor, flipped over, and slammed down again.

Mr. Slomin jumped back like he'd been burned. He goggled at the upside-down wreckage of his desk. Papers fluttered around it like butterflies. No one was laughing now.

I had to stop this before Mr. Slomin put two

and two together. I made a flying, nostril-pinching leap at Stan, but I was too late.

"A-choo!"

The front chalkboard melted into a thick gray liquid that oozed down the wall onto Mr. Slomin's shoes.

"Yikes!" Our teacher leaped out of the gooey puddle. You could still read the words *Current Events* in the mushy slop on his loafers.

"What's going on?" Calista quavered.

"Wait a minute." Mr. Slomin looked from Stan, to the puddle, and back to Stan again. "Every time *you* sneeze—"

Oh, no! Mr. Slomin had figured it out. The jig was up.

I felt my eyes well up with tears. Yeah, I know ☞ **Rule 2:** No crybabies. But even my rules of coolness didn't count anymore. The Air Force would take Stan away. Then we'd miss the deadline for sure! And poor Earth would be out past Pluto faster than you could shiver.

It was the end! There was no way out of this mess!

And then the bell rang.

Chapter 18

NOTHING COULD SAVE
US NOW

Stan and I headed for the door like we'd been shot out of a cannon.

"Hey!" called Mr. Slomin. "Come back here, you two!"

But a brick wall wouldn't have stopped us. We hurdled a couple of kindergarten kids and zoomed out the school yard gate.

I don't think all the power in the Crease could have gotten us home any faster. Sweating and gasping, we clattered up the front steps onto the porch.

"Safe!" Stan breathed.

"Not yet!" I wheezed. "Mr. Slomin's going to come after us!" My mind whirled. "You have to hide, and I'll say you took the bus back to Chicago!"

"Pan," he reminded me.

"Oh, whatever! Pan!"

The door opened, and my mom peeked out. "Hi, boys. Stan, you'll never guess what came for you in the mail today. You got something from—of all people—Leonardo DiCaprio! Did you write him a fan letter?"

I was hit by such a wave of relief that I almost fainted right there on the spot. Leonardo DiCaprio had come through with a new Panic Button! And we still had twenty minutes to come up with a slogan!

Mom handed Stan the envelope. "Now promise you'll share it with us at dinner." And she went back inside.

A bloodcurdling scream cut the air. *"Leee-ooo!"*

Onto the scene galloped my sister. She was followed by the seven other members of the Leonardo DiCaprio Fan Club, Clearview Chapter.

Lindsay snatched the letter right out of Stan's

hand. "It's true!" she shrieked. "This is *his* hand-writing! Leo touched this envelope! In person!"

"Give that back!" I snapped. "That's Stan's mail!"

But those eight girls were screaming so loud that I couldn't even hear myself.

I leaped forward and blocked the stairs. "Forget it, Lindsay! Give me that letter!"

And my sister—an innocent little first-grader—stomped on my foot so hard that I saw stars.

" Yeow! "

While I was hopping up and down in pain, all eight of them shoved right by me. They ran to the side yard and climbed the rope ladder to the tree house that was the fan club's headquarters. Lindsay pulled the ladder up after them.

Stan shook his head. "Lnrdnys has a startling effect on Earthling females. How odd. On Pan, he's considered an ugly duckling."

"Well, this is just great!" I exploded, dragging Stan over to the tree. I circled the thick trunk like a stalking panther. "If they open that letter, they'll probably lose the Panic Button! And

we've got no way to get up there and stop them!"

"Wait!" said my exchange buddy tensely. All at once, he began to bark.

"Aw, come on!" I urged. "In fifteen minutes, we turn into a planet of Popsicles! This is no time to call the dog!"

But Stan continued to yelp and growl. And when Fungus bounded up from the backyard, he and Stan talked things over.

Good old Fungus—
He grows on you.

"What is it?" I demanded.

"Neither of us can get into that tree house," my exchange buddy explained. "But Fungus can. I, Stan, have just made him a deputy agent of the Pan-Pan Travel Bureau. He'll get the letter for us."

"You're a genius!" I crowed. "You should have been a Smarty-Pant! You're a lot brighter than those two clowns who dropped Mom's mirror down a black hole!"

The fried-egg eyes turned tragic. "Alas, I, Stan, flunked out of Smarty-Pants University. I never figured out why manhole covers are round."

The plan was simple. Fungus jumped into my arms. Then Stan braced himself at the foot of the tree. I clambered up his back and sat on his shoulders. From there it was an easy reach. I raised Fungus over my head to the platform of the tree house. He climbed aboard, barking and wagging.

I heard Lindsay's friend Brittany exclaim, "Fungus! What a clever dog! You can climb trees!"

There was a lot of shuffling on the plywood floor as all the girls gathered around to pet Fungus.

"All right," said Lindsay. "This is the moment we've been waiting for. Let's open Leo's letter."

It all happened so fast that I'm amazed we weren't killed. I hoisted myself up a little and peered into the tree house. I was just in time to see Fungus snatch the letter right out of Lindsay's grasp.

"Fungus!"

Sixteen frantic hands made a grab for the dog. The letter clamped in his jaws, Fungus scrambled across the floor and took a flying leap into my arms. He tipped me, and I tipped Stan. The three of us—attached like one very tall person—toppled over backward.

"Oof!" We hit the ground like a ton of bricks. Fungus spat the letter into my hand and high-tailed it to his doghouse. Who ever said dogs are dumb animals?

The rope ladder came down off the tree house and smacked me right in the face. Lindsay led her crew over the side.

"Attack!" she roared.

Stan and I staggered to our feet and started running. Just as we approached the house, a car came speeding up to the curb. The door flew open, and out burst Mr. Slomin.

"Stop right there, Stan Mflxnys! I want a word with you!"

"Aw, no!" I howled.

What a way for this to end! We beat the clock! We had the Panic Button in our hands! It wasn't fair. We were so close. . . .

But nothing could save us now!

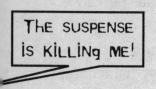

THE SUSPENSE IS KILLING ME!

Chapter 19

WHAT A SMALL UNIVERSE

As Mr. Slomin marched up to us, a little square window opened in the sky. A shiny object came hurtling straight down, whistling through the air.

Bonk!

It struck Mr. Slomin right on the top of the head. Our teacher took two wobbly steps and crumpled to the grass, unconscious.

I goggled at the item that had dropped out of nowhere.

"Mom's makeup mirror!" I exclaimed.

"Fascinating," said Stan. "The black hole of Cygnus X-1 lets out right over your house. What a small universe!"

"Ooooh!" groaned Mr. Slomin.

"He's starting to wake up!" I hissed. "Quick! Get that thing in your nose!"

Stan ripped open the letter, and there it was. I couldn't believe it! This Panic Button—this wondrous piece of technology—looked like half a grain of uncooked rice.

Stan handed me the letter. I barely dared to breathe while his steam shovel finger installed the replacement part.

There was a click, and the whir of a microwave oven.

How many nights had I lain awake, cursing that annoying noise? Now it was the most beautiful music in the world.

My exchange buddy beamed. "I, Stan, am back on-line."

"Quick!" I urged. "A slogan—"

And then the eight members of the Leonardo DiCaprio fan club caught up with the person who had their letter—me.

I won't try to sugarcoat it. They beat the daylights out of me. I know it's not very cool to get creamed by first-graders. But when you're outnumbered eight to one, at least you have an excuse.

ArE thEY a FaN CLUb Or a gOON SQUad?

130

"I give up!" I managed. "I surrender! Take the letter!"

Lindsay snatched the paper out of my hand. The other seven gathered around to hear the words of their idol.

"What does it say?" begged Brittany.

My sister began to read:

Dear Stan,
Take this and shove it up your nose.

Sincerely,
Leonardo DiCaprio

There was a shocked silence among the girls.

"Shove it up your nose?" Brittany repeated. "Why would Leo write such a mean letter?"

"This calls for an emergency fan club meeting," decided Lindsay. "Back to the tree house, everyone."

I looked at my watch. Three minutes to Pluto!

At that moment, Mr. Slomin woke up. He got to his feet and fixed Stan with blazing eyes.

"All right, Stan," he growled. "I'm wise to you.

The weird things happening around town are connected to your sneezing. Tell me what you know about the UFO sightings."

"Your suspicions are correct, Mr. Slomin," Stan began. "I, Stan, am—"

I stared at my buddy in horror. His eyes were crossed! We'd left the makeup mirror lying on the grass. Now it was glinting in his face! I dove on it and flipped it over.

"—a simple exchange student from Pan," he finished, eyes straight again.

"Oh, right. Pan," sneered Mr. Slomin. "I've looked in the atlas. There is no Pan outside Chicago. There's no Pan in any state. Now we're going to try a little experiment."

From his jacket pocket, he pulled out a pepper mill and ground it all over Stan's nose.

"A-*choo*!" sneezed my exchange buddy.

Mr. Slomin ducked like he was waiting for the lawn furniture to rise up and fly.

Nothing happened. Now that the nose computer was fixed, Stan's sneezes were completely harmless.

Mr. Slomin tried a little more pepper.

"A-*choo*! A-*choo*!"

Still nothing.

"Maybe you imagined it all," I suggested to our teacher.

Mr. Slomin was furious. He threw down his pepper mill in disgust and shook his finger at Stan. "I've got my eye on you, Mflxnys. You know more about this than you're saying." And he got into his car and squealed away, yelling threats about calling the Air Force.

I checked my watch again. My eyes almost popped out of my head. "Thirty seconds!" I howled. "Quick! Call the Smarty-Pants!"

"But we have no slogan," Stan protested.

"Call anyway! Fake it! Stall!"

Stan put his finger up his nose and made the transmission.

"This is Agent Mflxnys on Earth. I, Stan, have been off-line until this very moment. Do you read me?"

I held my breath. Seconds felt like hours. Finally, Stan flashed me thumbs-up. He had made contact.

All at once, he turned pale. "Earth's slogan? Yes, of course it's ready. The slogan is—uh—the slogan is—" He looked at me helplessly.

I don't know what made me do it. It was like my brain shut down, and my body snapped into action. I picked up the pepper mill and ground a black cloud of the stuff right in Stan's face.

"—the slogan is—a-*c h o o*!"

And then I heard a funny sound. It took me a moment to realize it was coming out of Stan's nose. It was—I strained to listen—cheering! Applause! Shouts of "Bravo!"

Unbelievable! These were voices from eighty-five thousand light-years away, on Pan!

"Yes, you can believe your ears," Stan said to them. "That was sneezation. It's just one of the fabulous vacation activities on Earth. That's my slogan, 'a-*choo.*' I, Stan, defy Shkprnys to do any better."

I looked at my watch and allowed myself to start breathing again. We beat the deadline by two seconds!

"We made it, right?" I squeaked. "We're not getting whooshed past Pluto?"

Stan was weak with relief. "The Smarty-Pants have agreed to do extra study on both planets before a decision is made on the new tourist spot. Earth is still in the running!"

"Hah!" I celebrated. "In your face, Shakespeare! Your brilliant slogan lost to a sneeze!"

"I've got to file an official report immediately," Stan announced.

And there, right on my front lawn, he dug his finger further up his nose than ever before. It was a steam shovel job big enough to uncover an underground city. He was working the controls of his nasal processor so fast and so hard that I could see his arm muscles bulging through his white dress shirt.

"Stan, not here!" I rasped. "The whole neighborhood can see you! Wait till we get inside!"

Stan dropped his hand guiltily. "I'm sorry," he said in his saddest munchkin voice. "After all your flash cards and all your help, I, Stan, have once again acted like a dweeb. No wonder I have no title. I can't do anything right." He was so dejected that he couldn't even look me in the eye. "I'm an embarrassment to you, Devin. I, Stan, will never become cool."

It was the very first moment I realized that I wouldn't trade Stan for a hundred Codys and Wandas and Sams. The luckiest day of my life was the day he came rolling down that baggage chute!

I clamped a hand on his skinny shoulder. "I just made up a new rule of coolness, and this is the

I FEEL warm and FUZZY all over.

136

most important one of all: ☛ Saving the planet automatically cancels out every dweeby thing you've ever done. So you are cool. You want a title? From now on, you are Mflxnys, the Totally Cool."

He got all misty-eyed. "Devin—you honor me! I feel like a child of eighty again! To sneeze and be cool, both in the same week! I, Stan, am so excited I could go to the dentist!"

Okay, so I lied about Stan being cool. But there was no better exchange buddy—not in eighty-five thousand light-years!